FONDNESS
ENVY

SUMEET KUMAR

Copyright © Sumeet Kumar
All Rights Reserved.

This book has been published with all efforts taken to make the material error-free after the consent of the author. However, the author and the publisher do not assume and hereby disclaim any liability to any party for any loss, damage, or disruption caused by errors or omissions, whether such errors or omissions result from negligence, accident, or any other cause.

While every effort has been made to avoid any mistake or omission, this publication is being sold on the condition and understanding that neither the author nor the publishers or printers would be liable in any manner to any person by reason of any mistake or omission in this publication or for any action taken or omitted to be taken or advice rendered or accepted on the basis of this work. For any defect in printing or binding the publishers will be liable only to replace the defective copy by another copy of this work then available.

Sumeet Kumar

Sumeet Kumar , A adult who experiences many phases of life , a well known writer and a writer of new era . In reality he is a writter as well as singer (as a hobby) and a standup comedian . Very exciting and interesting fact about him is that he is author of New era i.e. he starts his journey of writing at the age when he was going to schools to get the study . His streak of 100 books will be the great achievement for him in future. His some famous works i.e.

Maturity Of Love (Genre - Love),Privacy For Dream (Genre - Middle Class), Army Squad ofLove (Genre- The Seperation of Army Love), 5 Days of Love(Genre- Temporarily Love), Th e Endearment Of Love(Genre - Historical Era Of Love), Social Destruction Indo-Pak (Genre - The Story of The Love At The Time Of Division Of India And Pakistan), Middle Class Soul (Genre - The Dreams of Middle Class), The Accursed Kanatpur (Genre -The Horrific Story Of A Village), Wrong Number (Genre -The Suspenseful Physco Killer Story), The Secrecy OfDeadly Midnight (Genre - The Suspense About a Crime),Fragile Religious Of Death (Genre- The Death Of A TrustfulPerson), Nature Vs Science (Genre - The Future Battle Between Nature And Science In A Horrific Way), Generic Man (Genre - The Dream of I.I.T), The Unconsious 12 Hours(Genre - The Illusion At Stage Of Comma), The StrangeBurden (Genre - The Burden Of Love) , Her Existence (Genre- The Female Pain In The Society) , Jockstrap Prize (Genre -The True Story Of A National Athlete) , H Man [Hindi] (Genre - Superhero Tragic Story), H Man [English] (Genre - Superhero Tragic Story) , Maturity Of Love [Englsih] (Genre - Love) and many more are available on various geners on the offcial platform of **Amazon, Flipkart and Notionpress**. You can buy them from there.

Contents

Acknowledgements   *vii*

1. Lost In A Strange World   1

2. The Demanding Sacrifice   7

3. In-depth Feeling   14

ACKNOWLEDGEMENTS

Aman Kumar

Special Thanks to **Aman Kumar** who worked so hard in the preparation of this book. He has continually put with my passive voice, omission of words, and late night calls. You have been wonderful. Thanks to him for his precious time in reviewing proposals , individual chapters and early drafts, along with his suggestions on the applicability of the material to the world.

I

Lost In A Strange World

Whatever condition I am in today, it is only because of me, I do not know the exact reason for it at all I do not even know who I am undefined with what importance I have come to the world, undefined feet, my thinking makes me feel all the time. it was saying that now the love of living is not that long, why am I feeling like this, I have every witness with whom I love every hope that can give a new hope to my dreams, then who is right? It is said that my body is separating me all the time. Nor is it important that when we say goodbye to our own fear, is it a husband without our companions that he too would have adopted the word of the path somewhere? It is to live to die, this is the shadow of good luck, which God has created in one day, the thoughts come within me, if there is humanity in the world, then who taught humanity, if there is a word of happiness, then who is the rain of sorrow That whatever time is present, why is he not with him, he says to stay close, why is his love of the heart and feet is not clear nowadays, why could he never do what I think, would his troubles end by the time when we are on his side Moving forward, she would go somewhere far away from us, about which we never even think about what fate has to accept, I don't know what my feet are. I need someone else's support, I myself can carry forward the desire of my life, I can recite it again to return to myself, then why am I fostering such a spirit, from whom I say to stay away from I say to stay till my words, I tell to keep silent inside myself, why I am not able to keep up why I have to move towards someone when all of them Has given relationships toads, has given many deceits, has changed his nature every time, so why can't I change then why I worry about those who say to go away from my life, they say to stay apart. Why do I look at him, is it true, what compulsions are making me look towards him, what do I say to myself, every rude bash advises me to stay away from them, yet when I go to them, why can't I say anything? Who has been imprisoned in my part, whose arguments have taken me as a criminal, considering myself wrong and have told the path many times, God has never accepted my love, nor has it ever accepted my dream. The door of education has been given in my hands, if I say that I can be very difficult myself, is it right? Every time I worry about those people who have started saying to hate me, only I have started rioting after my beating. I don't know what is the mistake I have done, in reality, my love for people is not wrong because the witness who has shown his self. Take the man has been involved in the courtroom and has asked many questions, how can his love be right.

"e a traveller
But didn't get a destination in life
I don't own a love
neither a way to get peace in lifeI becom"

..My condition is such that even my feet can't say trustworthiness, I can't even say that I'm right and I don't even know the reason for this. I try to find myself, I run after them, try to share with them, I also tell the tradition of their coming to go, feet they neither mention telling the story nor the conspiracy to ever go ahead with the tradition of asking I do everything is right, even those logs in life who hate me and those people from whom I have started telling every day to stay apart, I do not know how long my companions will be with me, how will I ask this question every time? Am I ready to walk with me? Without explaining your love, how can his love be wrong. I should fulfill this desire, I should separate myself so much that it should never be exhibited again, nor is my rudeness ruining me so much that I can't make him settle again even by saying that, I have broken in front of myself. So how to take care of myself: I can't understand why I get tired every time my feet are on the floor where my life is only difficult for me, why do I want relationships to protect myself, is it okay to be alone? My happiness is work party, my anger for my anger is also such a love, from which neither we can ever separate ourselves like unfaithful nor can we say it to hurt ourselves because the day this fanna comes to the fore Gone each day the road will carry our luck together, I have said to myself thousands of times that it is over, then why are you saying such words, do you still have any wishes, people say that this life is only once You get the truth, it is said that you get this life only once, forget all your sorrows by hashing it and try to move forward, it is a lie by sacrificing the pain every day. After achieving smile, I can't even say that my soul will come back for a few days, and that happiness too, because I don't even know my own destiny, who will show me the right kind of devotion, I will go ahead and feel sorry. Even then, I will do some charity foot, my love foot, which I had asked for my own charity every time. I am also telling myself about the fear and also the tradition of eradicating it, after all I am trying to attach myself to such an expectation which will probably not be pure, it can be finish everything in a moment I am able to move forward and I am starting to like this foot too, now this silence is lonely Why didn't I know why I didn't feel with me, what is the name of a poison for every one of his affections, in his gathering, which I have tried to drink, it is a matter of hearing all this. Maybe my love is not feeling well for everyone I am the first person in the world who is troubled by my own self, I understand my feet, yet I am surprised, the love of the heart will give every time, I am still ready to stop myself, no one understands me, I do not understand I am the one who is great in myself. Maybe you all are not understanding my words, I know this thing, even a few days ago, I was away from them, I was living an exotic life of my own and maybe also happy then my life I made an entry, which I understood that she is the world's best woman, only a few days later the news came that she is the world's out-of-syllabus story, undefined, in which I do not want to listen to the sad story of my life first because I know that Nowadays, in our world, it has many problems, that means the trend has started and you must have heard many news related to it, so you all have to wear dark clothes. The foot that is not taken in the world at all, his story is also good, first look at the side mirror, all because this is the story of Rihan Rastogi, you all must also be thinking that why am I talking like this, there is a story of what to do. What is going to come out after some time, till then there is a show of waiting for a little bit. By the way, my name is Rohit Rastogi and the one we are going to tell you about is none other than our sweet and priest brother, meaning we are his younger brother, by the way, his life is a complete comedy, feet say that the life of a hero is absolutely true Silent like the moon and even single feet, there was no such thing in our brother, that means he used to be silent, all the time the feet have not remained single till today. Let's do two or four words in abuses and do every soft candle night dinner.After that, only we will see all of them, therefore, I keep love away from it by making salvation, it is not such a thing that we have never fallen in love with anyone, we also love feet, that is only the cashew cutter that Kaam Pandey belongs to. This nurturing foot is found every evening, God says true, what is the magic in his hands, undefined, we can't handle ourselves and eat one kilo of cashew nut every day, it is another matter that the problem of acidity in the stomach It happens that even the father-in-law says that it is not a wonderful thing, he destroys life all the time and his example is to see the life of our brother, by the way, we also take something, we are not so proud that our locality understands us. And do not talk about mother, dad mother-in-law till today, we have not got any respect for us. Somebody looks like a morsel, hey artist, we have a little bit of explaining to them, by the way, we love our mother very much, what to do is the only thing like love if in life If there is any wealth, it is only because of mother's love and the rest keeps on coming, we neither have to do anything big nor become big, yet there is a saying in the heart that even when we die, our mother son is in front of our eyes. Only if we see it, we will be able to go upstairs and enjoy heaven, in the same way, the legs should not be too much, because now the whole story is told. There is a search for the destination, just complete each of its paths, before listening to the Kahirish story, before narrating it, the first request is that those with a weak heart should stay away from it, and especially those people who are bitten by love's feet every two days. They go and they shed their tears all the time, but life is alive and will continue to be so, let us tell you the whole story for then, if we meet again sometime undefined.

> *"Here meaning of dream is changed*
> *I love someone who has changed*
> *I have something left over me*
> *By when i am turning back in my life i saw*
> *everything has changed"*

II
The Demanding Sacrifice

It is said that faith is the reason for which many people
have been sacrificed and many are still waiting to see when
we get this disease and when we get self-liberation, love
teaches people to live, nor had I heard anywhere, never saw

feet. It turned out to be like our death. India, which does good deeds, never shows its year in the form of a gift, in the same way, there is no talk of spoiling the name, we had a request to take something including the feet, so the name was used for the purpose. It was necessary, it is not our story, it cannot even be said that even though we are not our story, I mean to say that even though it is our story, the feet with whom we are connected are ours, we mean the caresses of our homes and of our dad, Dear also good till now you guys could not understand whose words I am doing, it is none other than our dear revered brother Rihan Rastogi who has not done any wrong from childhood till today and look at us one is absolutely hated. We, who keep doing wrong things all the time, it is not at all such a thing that we are not fair, what should our feet do, no one will know and our sorrows. Da never go, first we tell that neither we are fans of Tiger Shroff nor do we know him, his father likes us, that's why we also like him very much, well these words will continue to happen before that we are our elders. Brother Rihan please do something obvious about Rastogi and about your family, although the length of our family is enough, we mean to say that our dad has earned a lot of name, there is no mistake in that too. Means we are doing the things of brother Rihan Rastogi, he did such things which he can do which is absolutely a bookworm, so listen, we call him bookworm eyes, for the first time when our dad got admission of both of us, then a few months later It is our brother who became the teacher of the school, how did it mean so soon: there is no need to bring the undefined mind to a confused state, let us tell how he became a student with a teacher? So the matter was such that our brothers I was a big fan of reading sir, that too since childhood and Bauji used to like him a lot earlier. It was because he was also their first son and was worth everything for everything else, we were absolutely opposite to him. my prince brother used to do Rihan Rastogi ws complex min about their future and the past which we felt every day like a present, Dad knew very well that if he taught Rihan brother good health, then he became a very big man one day. It would be that if such a desire seems strange to us, then we get undefined boy education, then why did our babuji think that he will make his son a good person by reading and writing, it is not that our dad has a profession. There was a lack of paiseh toh timbe, even sitting and eating our eight books, the feet were not the respect that our dad used to say since childhood, there is a long story behind it too See what such scandals he has done, because of which we have got wealth, but by keeping our feet respectful. Babar, then this story is of 1966 when our grandfather Amal Azad Tyagi was alive, he was in great fear in our city, people were very afraid of him because at that time he used to be the head of some organization and he was not a minor head nor anyone. He was the head of the accessory, he was the head of an organization whose slogans were enough, there is no need to go around like this to scare the logo and to continue the fear, we never thought of what we should do. Was that our grandfather was such a courageous person first and don't give gifts to the brave because our babuji says that he had killed a lion alive, that too with the help of his Kaveri, he was like pure in words but if there was a kind kf revenge its became a hell king , his work and thoughts were there is completely different means Kaveri is neither a dharna of any river nor a friend's grandfather never used to separate his Kaveri from himself, he used to say that the day it broke, my mother-in-law also left, that's why our Grandfather never used to keep his Kaveri separate from himself, by the way, the organization he was heading had only one slogan and its words were in some way. Were undefined to shed blood and earn money undefined means that you must have gone to the feet of your ears because when our dad told us about these batis, that too about our grandfather, we also thought on a happy day that we too should be our grandfather Just like phantom humans will be made and a great organization will be formed, what should the feet do, this population was not acceptable to us, it is not that they did not shed the blood of the poor, they used to flow their blood as much as the feet of the rich. Because of some deceit, his life remains alive only when the clue and lamp of the cheater are both handy, all the logs were with him, he loved Grandfather very much and considered him as his Sardar and Grandfather also supported him. Never left, he also raised them like his family and read his children because he was a great student, he was also a great student of mathematics, his condition was not good for some time and he was healthy in front of his eyes at the time of such an accident. It happened that even without saying their rudeness, they were forced to change their feet, what is the truth of it or neither we know nor our children.dad has never mentioned to us, he never used to leave the side of his men who were loyal to him. Grandfather could even die for him. For those who were not loyal to him, his Kaveri was enough, in the same way, we did his work. Told about her feet, there was no discussion about her life that Kaveri was the name of our grandmother, whom our grandfather loved like Romeo and Juliet, however, his story took a morr when Dadima's babuji took our grandfather's name. Very insulting to father because his father was a blacksmith at the time and our grandmother's father was a blacksmith, that means what pair did the above person make of him and his family's "blacksmith" on one side and on the other side" "blacksmith" means that if their profession is tested with eyes, then there is no reason to say any difference between them, which should be taken to the fore because both do the work of hard work, one seeks the other and yet the fear of the other is undefined. Don't know the whole story, you can tell as much as your feet, you all have more scope for questions and answers only then. It will be complete when their story progresses, Well when Grandmother's father had insulted our Grandfather's father, on this day Grandfather had thought that he would bring grandmother to his house only when he would be capable of her and she had to sleep. Sitting in the doli, how he would bring his feet, he had neither told himself nor his father and before that he went to heaven even before he told anything to his father, he too was suffering from cholera, after all. Humar Grandfather's dreams were broken, his feet were still hanging in his Kaveri, which he used to love very much, meaning our grandmother, when grand mothercame to know about this, then at that time she was coming to meet Grandfather that his father had Took them rock and after that many wadas told to accept and keep the same old drama who do father of a girl in every fourth house that if you cross the threshold you will see our dead mouth what was after that grandma became a bit sent And he broke the dam inside his threshold only one day, meaning he killed the soul, after that the war that started was such that Even my words are a little nervous to say this, when Grandfather came to know that his Kaveri is no longer in the world, then the storm of anger which was growing inside him for a long time was also about the society. what was not to happen, in the end, the same thing happened, I do not know how true and how many false feet tell me to say it, what I say to say love is the wall that keeps every witness away from cruelty. The day when its limit is broken, humiliation also takes place in front of us. Grandfather never thought that he would become a poor man, the limit of luck could not save his love, and while saying no, Grandfather did what he probably did. Wasn't right, to be honest, Grandpa had no enmity before anyone, the day his Kaveri died, that means, my grandmother, on the happy day, he had taken this life that he would hang the neck of his culprit by cutting the neck. Where his Kaveri had spent the last moments and that was the reality too, I mean to say, Grandfather did what he said, in the end Whom did I sacrifice? How did it happen and who killed him? Grandfather these batons did not know at all who killed his Kaveri. And maybe even the feet of his entire family, I do not find these batis true, what is the truth of it, today neither then father has told nor I have ever dared to ask how even grandfather died, we are right now It is very difficult because whenever we ask our babuji this, he drives us away by calling us Topa, he tries to beat us together with his nursery behind us and every time we get out of sight and he has no ears. The news does not seem to be there. Now I am in the mood to go, so sorry, the story is not only incomplete but it is very incomplete because we have lost it. Just stepped on the whole story in my gathering, so now Chand Seh is also difficult. We knew that our babuji would never tell us about Grandfather, so we thought that we should not ask our mother to think about it, whose name is border Rastogi. That our life is the most important person in our small right world, it is not such a thing that we do not know English, our father-in-law is very young in speaking feet, that's why we do not speak when we asked our mother-in-law, she also said something about grandfather enough did not tell special things, he said so much that our father-in-law and your grandfather also died where his Kaveri died. It is because father did not tell anything about his mother, we mean about our Grandmother.

"God i want a glimpse of you
Because here everywhere i saw that there is a
fake identity of you."

III

In-Depth Feeling

By the way, there have been so many turns in our life, the feet which it was supposed to be, maybe it was too much, that means because of the way we keep running away from childhood, in the end, it becomes our destination and it also comes in front of us and collides with us and our life. So many such destinations have come and gone, even then Rihan Rastogi's life hit such a turn that he forgot his own path, meaning our brother Jaan, who was a scholar since childhood, has now become a double scholar, even if someone's love I. So eight years ago, I asked everyone to walk the peach a little, on the last day his life was knocked like that right now, so that his life is not taking the name of life, I had already told that Grandpa's Black status means to remove the evil shadow and to lane the lost respect of our family, our dad got both of us to Admission on that kind of school where he hoped that we will come to make some big feet that I heard the story Meaning, I did not find anything wrong about my grandfather that he did something wrong by killing his enemies, after all he Nase their love was Chinese, so I think Rastogi family persons didn't like then , long ago because Grandfather had also killed a brahmin and why was undefined because of this we were still ignorant So fear was that our people used to respect our babuji out of fear because dad had done many scandals, in the same way, if I talk about myself, then this limit will be repeated again because we also had to be like our grandfather, we have absolutely fearless feet. dad didn't say this at all, that's why he even left the fire where Grandfather's soul broke the dam, meaning where Grandfather died, feet say that the future can change, feet are not the shadow of the past, so now the whole story of the Rastogi family begins. To play the role of interpretation, the journey we are about to take is going to happen, please tie your enough bags.

MANDERA CHUNGI ALLAHABAD
NOVEMBER 2002

Means today is the day when I and Rihan brothers have gone on such a journey to fulfill their duty where I can neither see my destination nor the feet of our Rihan brothers, whose happiness has no place, the age of both of us is only There is a limit of three years, it means that I am not the smallest in my house, I am not even big, my ride is in the middle, there is also a small child whose name is Karthik Rastogi. We can't say anything about our repentance, feet are our dad life, because those who are small, go ahead and see how the first day started at the end: that too the school of science where my mind desires this answer all the time. I was giving now running away, now I can not feel this pain because some things were like this because I was new and my friendship was not at all I used to carry a weapon in my pocket because I had to be like Grandpa, I had forgotten in my feet that Grandpa was also a good student. They were also on the other side of mathematics and on the other hand, my talk was different because neither the party nor the English would have expelled me from the world of mathematics if I had run my enough like many schools and their managment had done me before. And enough was a small reason behind this, that I used to carry more books and weapons in my school bags and what kind of weapons they were, you all must be understanding that I had a great hobby since childhood that log mujseh bhi scared me too Be afraid, no one has ever taken my feet seriously, first my life took it, then my babuji and after all the whole understanding, so all the killers of grandfather, he used to keep them with him, that too hidden from the eyes of everyone. In today's time, someone's hard work can be hidden, no one's girl is at all, after leaving eight schools, this was my ninth school, where neither my thinking was found nor my hair was well Rihan brother ,maybe settled in the school on the very first day and scholars were not a matter of jealousy in the eyes of everyone because Rastogi was It was a problem that we never used to fight with each other, that's why I didn't have any problem with their relationship and I'm telling their stories in new words, that means their whole story feet are true that in 17 years they never told me. I didn't even talk and what is the reason behind this, I don't even stand, he is the eldest in our house and says as I have mentioned earlier, it is said that only a good person kills him, feet in my part. So the bailout of both was frequent, good and evil, even though dad used to beat us all the time, he always let me feel whenever he said two words, he used to cry himself and we also made us cry, meaning our relationship was completely beyond science. Many times people also used to say that I am not even their own beta, maybe this thing can be wrong, we also used to feel my feet, well my relationship was my own and there is no malefic in my loved ones. By the way, Rihan brother completely, He was not only famous in school because he was a scholar, he knew many other things because of which people respected him. And used to stay away from us, all the teachers liked him very much, no such assembly passed where we did not listen to his praise, every day, every time and everyone used to resonate in everyone's speech, there is no student like Rihan. I am remembering the reason for an accident in school which is very related to me and even though we didn't have baatis at all, the name identity and then it was famous in the whole school and our locality, we in identify named ushi. On the other hand, everyone was infamous for saying that Rastogi has three boys, in which two are okay, one is a devil, so the accident about which I am going to mention was in some way, when I accidentally collided with the principal of the school and when there was a collision between both of us and then collided with him in such a way that he broke his leg and the confusion that followed was in some way.

CONVERSATION

"**ME** : *oh sorry sir undefined i used to say not to ask you small.*

PRINCIPAL : *Owl's straps, you gave my feet toad (vaping mode undefined Oh Amma, I will throw you out of school, you are an asshole, what can't you see? The whole school is famous for its education and on the other hand, those who are not taking the name of improvement undefined To be honest, I didn't do it at all by sacrificing my feet, as my words were coming out, I was saying that I should have given a today by arming my life, what can the feet do, now what is already decided, we can not change it.*"

Even saying no, I did what I should not have done, all the stuff in the school and the children, all of them got together and started speaking the words which I had been hearing since long ago, my little attention is being paid. I had gone so that he ran away without telling that too because I knew what was going to happen next, dad was beaten up again with angry eyes and then he left the school, then undefined in another school, all this was public undefined Rihan brother was also standing still, he didn't say anything, that bash he was numb in everyone's and everyone's just blaming, I was mixing, in that he was too happy that even the batis were numb and everyone else I have gone across the border, so I don't say that, even though I have to go, dad didn't say anything to us, nor mother , who meant the silence that was right in my mind by turning me into poison. Jahar bann hi thi mother even tried to talk, she did not give any answer.On this day two things came to my mind that the little ones who don't look like murders, they seem like little loved ones. Babuji always understood us whenever we did any wrong thing. The day we broke the feet of our principal;

I had also done that in front of us, which we can neither do nor adopt to express our selfishness, after a man's day, my indignation took this that I am wrong, so after the day I had those dreams too. This fact I left him and that house also there are some roads which lead towards the destination, feet never make them aware, I knew that to remove the stain, Babuji has worked so hard, I need to grow more. I'm trying, after all, it was such a night on which I could neither sleep nor relax because when they had a stopper party, neither all the tears also used to work like ointments, when they did not understand me nor did they understand me. Nor did I ask anything because I had understood that the story of trouble is something else. dad should not have any problem because of us, so on this day he has only two sons, first our Rihan Bhai and secondly our little prince of our house. After this day, it has been almost five years, we had some arrows, so we left that square When we returned back to those abuses, their air had also changed completely and when we used to have our shelter in the four walls of the house, then its strings were also touched by the hands, why are these batons saying what is the meaning. Baatis are like that, perhaps you all will remain secretive, your feet will be like this, when we returned home, it was nothing, neither our dad shop nor the house to which my childhood memories were connected, they were all the same. In the moment, she had also disappeared from my eyes Even after he went to school, no one answered, he refused to believe that even a boy named Rihan used to study this and I also did not have records. After all, in five years, what is the right thing that happened to my family that even a small child of their existence is not visible in front of my eyes that it is okay undefined I didn't even know if my family is fine then that Where is everything, Dad mother brother and Sehjda? secrets bailout is a bit long and my story is still incomplete even after being complete, my happiness in the words of destruction has been lost, I can't tell it because there are so many feet on the way, my destination is still there.

"I have earned many thing in my life
which is not more but not less
i want to live more
to make my dream to reality
I know that nothing is permanent
but my mom and dad is alone without me
I want to live more
to make my dream to reality
I want to be a person like my dad
I want to take all the blessing by him
I want to live more
to make my dream to reality
I want to let my past down
to be better
I want to live more

to make my dream to reality"

to make my dream to reality"

www.ingramcontent.com/pod-product-compliance
Lightning Source LLC
Chambersburg PA
CBHW021158130726
47988CB00004B/1665